UP THE WOODEN HILL

A COLLECTION OF SHORT STORIES

NANCY WIEDMAN

Published by Happy Jack Publishing, LLC

Copyright © June 2017
by Nancy Wiedman

Cover design by Tina Lampe

Author Photo by Kathryn Lauer

ISBN: 1-944104-13-5
ISBN-13: 978-1-944104-13-9

DEDICATION

To my daughters, Kathryn Lauer, and Mary Steed

.

CONTENTS

ACKNOWLEDGMENTS

I would like to thank the splendid staff at Happy Jack Publishing Company; especially Beth Burgmeyer, editor/publisher, who carefully prepared my collection of short stories for publication.

.

UP THE WOODEN HILL

G rammy lived on the corner of Fifteenth and Pine Streets in a double house on the outskirts of Berwick, Pennsylvania with my Aunt Fae, her youngest daughter, who was an elementary schoolteacher. Helen and Tiny lived on the other side of the house, which my grammy inherited after Grandpa's death in 1929. Tiny was anything but Tiny, nor was his wife. Years later, though, after World War II, when Tiny returned from the Army, I saw a picture of the couple. Between them, they must have lost over 100 pounds, and were almost unrecognizable in their transformed svelteness.

Grammy and Aunt Fae's house had a front porch with a swing. The back porch was where the wringer washer was kept. On Saturday's, wash days, a hose was strung through the pantry window to the faucets at the sink to be filled with water. Clothes were hung, summer and winter, outdoors on lines to dry.

As a child, and in fact until 1948, my family and I spent most Christmases at Grammy's. I often spent two weeks or more of summer vacation there as well. I usually traveled by train with Mother from the junction of the New York Central and Lehigh Valley railroads to Wilkes Barre. Dad would join us later for a week and the trip home by car.

The first time I went to Grammy's alone I was eight years old. My parents put me on a train, briefed me again on behavior and safety issues, handed me my shoebox lunch, and kissed me goodbye.

Before I could exit the train in Wilkes Barre, my uncle Jesse, Mother's brother, boarded with the conductor, who asked me if I knew this man. "Well of course," I said. "He's my Uncle Jesse." The conductor and my uncle seemed highly amused by my answer.

The summer I was twelve, after a serious bout with pneumonia, and somehow making it through seventh grade, my mother handed me money instead of the usual box lunch. "This time," she said, "you will have lunch in the dining car." What a treat and surprise this was.

The steward came through the car at noon with chimes announcing lunch time. There was a special menu for young people. I chose the grilled cheese sandwich, which came with a dill pickle and potato chips, and chocolate ice cream for dessert. I had been taught about leaving a tip, which at that time, was 10 percent.

Today, over sixty years later, I could draw a picture of Grammy's house. There was a parlor with a hardly used sofa, French style chairs, a coffee table, lamps, desk, and piano. The front door had a letter slot, and when the postman arrived, one of a long succession of dogs, from Beauty to Penny and finally, Ginger, would retrieve the mail and carefully deliver it to Grammy's lap, where she sat in an oak rocking chair (of a morning), in the sitting room. That room had an old couch, a library table, telephone, round oak dining table and chairs. A deer head with sad brown eyes was mounted on one wall, complete with hooves for hanging hats, and a mirror.

The kitchen was most interesting to me. I'd never seen anything like it. There was a coal stove where Grammy did all the cooking. She baked bread every week, which I didn't really appreciate at the time. I missed good old Wonder Bread. At home, we had an electric refrigerator. Grammy had an icebox with a pan underneath it that had to be emptied as the ice melted—my job in the summer. There was an old glass front china cabinet, table and chairs, all painted apple green, which I figured was Grammy's favorite color, since it was repeated in her bedroom furniture upstairs. The pantry had a bread box where one could usually find a stale slice of bread or sweet roll. The sink was made of tin.

At about the same time every night, Grammy would say that she was going up the wooden hill, an expression I didn't immediately catch onto. Later, I realized that it was a pretty good metaphor for climbing stairs.

During the day, I often climbed one more flight up the wooden hill to the attic, which was filled with treasures from the past. Grandpa's violin with its broken strings hung on the wall. There was a large doll, a cradle, high chair, table and chairs, and a child's china tea set.

A steamer trunk held old clothing: Uncle Walter's size 13 outdated brown oxfords, Aunt Kathryn's starched nurse's uniform and shoes, and curiously, a child's beige fur coat. I was told it was to be mine someday. At first, it was too large; eventually too small, and I never got to wear it.

My bedroom was the middle room up the wooden hill. From my window, I could see Smith's grocery store, illuminated by a street light in front.

Across the street from Grammy's, there were chickens, and a rooster crowed every morning at 6 a.m. No need for an alarm clock in that neighborhood. The little boy, Brickie, who lived in that house, had red hair—just like the rooster.

Grammy would have described herself as a country woman, having grown up on a farm. Most of her friends were country women too. They were not fancy folks, in other words, and certainly without pretentions. So, it seems strange, in a way, that they observed a formality when speaking to each other. Grammy was Mrs. Bonham to her friends, and they were Mrs. Wright and Mrs. Beaver. Those women visited Grammy, or she stopped at their houses frequently. Mr. Bowes was a long-time family friend. When Grandpa died, Mr. Bowes, who owned a nice car, would drive Grammy to a club she belonged to named appropriately, The Widows.

In Berwick, I had many summer friends: June, daughter of the owner of Smith's grocery, Joan, whose parents had a bakery, and Shirley. Shirley's father drove a store on wheels to rural areas during the week. Sometimes on Saturdays, he would let Shirley and her friends choose snacks from the store and we would have a party on the porch.

June Smith's grandfather, who lived next to the store, also owned a farm where he kept an antique stagecoach and horses. One day, June told me that her grandfather was bringing the coach and team and she could invite a couple of friends to come along for a ride. I jumped at the chance—my first and only ride in a stagecoach. We pretended to be actors in a western movie—never mind the bumps and dust!

Through many years not much changed, until everything did. Grammy sold her house. She and Aunt Fae moved to a warmer climate.

In memory, I often go up the wooden hill. This time, though, I do not run up the steps, but hold on to the railing as I had been taught to do.

THE LAST DANCE

Some of the girls in Jane's class had attended every prom since seventh grade. That meant a new gown every year for the past five years. It was an important school event, of course, and it meant that the invitees were popular.

Jane never had never been invited to a prom. She was pretty sure it was because she was a little on the plump side. But now that she had lost twenty pounds, and it was her senior year, maybe her luck would change. It was the last chance for her to go.

Coming home from school one day, she heard a familiar voice call her name. "Jane, wait up," Tom O'Brien said. "I want to ask you something."

Tom probably didn't hear the Latin assignment, for a change, Jane thought. He never seemed to be awake during class.

"Hey, if you don't already have a date for the prom, would you go with me?" He couldn't seem to get the words out fast enough.

"I don't have a date, and I'd like to go with you," Jane said.

"Okay, good. We can ride with Bob and Ellen. Talk to you later."

Jane's heart was beating so fast. She couldn't wait to tell Mom. "This is wonderful, Jane. See, I told you this would happen. We will have to go shopping—maybe on Saturday. I get paid on Friday."

That's when Jane had second thoughts about the dance. Money was scarce, especially since Dad had lost his job and the only money coming in was Mom's pay from her teaching job in the local elementary school.

On Saturday, though, Jane and her mother rode the bus to the nearby city. It didn't take long for Jane to find a dress she liked. It was strapless, pink taffeta, with beading on the bodice. Jane's mother looked at the price tag the first thing, and she could see by the expression on her mother's face that it would be way over budget.

But Mother, who more than anything wanted her daughter to have a beautiful gown for her prom, figured the family could eat Spam and tomato soup for a while. The dress was purchased, as well as silver pumps and a small evening purse.

The prom would be in three weeks. When Aunt Sylvia, who owned a hair salon, heard the news about Jane's date, she offered to style her hair and do her makeup for the occasion.

Jane's friends were happy to hear that she was going to the dance with Tom. And, it was fun to be part of the prom-going crowd.

But, a week before the prom, Jane got a call from Tom. "Jane, I hate to tell you this, but I have to break our date. I hope you understand. It's a family situation."

Jane was stunned. Her hopes of going to the last dance were over. The expensive dress her mother really couldn't afford was unreturnable. Poor Tom, she thought. It must be bad—a family problem he can't talk about.

How would she tell her mother that going to the prom was out. Prom clothes had been a waste of money.

But after supper that night, Jane told her mother. "Honey, I'm so sorry about this. But, it's not your fault, and probably not Tom's either, if there are family problems."

Jane hoped to keep the news quiet, but the next day, everybody in school seemed to know. Actually, they knew a lot more about it than Jane did.

One of her friends told her that Tom asked someone else when he learned that the girl he thought had a date was free.

That night, when Jane came home from school, she got a call from a boy named Jim. He was in her Latin class, and so shy that she had never talked to him.

"I know this is last minute, Jane, but would you consider going to the prom with me?"

It seemed that he was feeling sorry for her, and Jane was hesitant to accept. When she mentioned it, Jim assured her that while he knew she had been stood up, he had always wanted to ask her for a date. Tom's bad behavior gave him the opportunity and courage to act, he said.

The night of the prom, Jim arrived at the door with a corsage of pink roses. Jane was surprised that she had never noticed how handsome Jim was. His shyness, too, seemed to have vanished almost overnight.

Going to the prom, the last dance of her last year in school, was a dream come true for Jane.

There were two people missing from the dance—Tom and his date, Maureen, who had been infected with measles.

THE SIGN PAINTER'S DAUGHTER

It was a night for howling wolves and polar bears, with temperatures hovering just above zero; blizzard conditions. Nobody with any sense would be walking six miles in the dark, wearing clothing that was inadequate for the weather, to deliver ads to a store. Nobody that is, except a man who needed money: a hungry man, a family man, a poor sign painter.

The year was 1934—the height of The Great Depression. The sign painter, whose name was Jim, had lost his job at the mill. He was trying to make a living by painting signs and lettering trucks. They were poor—he and his wife, Doretta, and their little daughter, Dena.

"Jim, it's no disgrace to be poor," Doretta often said.

"Maybe not, but it's darned inconvenient," Jim would say.

Then they would both laugh, and agree half-heartedly that it couldn't last forever.

Snow seemed to be coming down faster, and drifting across the highway. At least there were no cars on the road. But Jim was only halfway to his destination. He held his coat closer, protecting the rolled-up paper signs. To pass the time, he thought of the Christmas season, about to begin. It made him happy and sad at the same time. Little two-year-old Dena asked the Santa at the local department store for only one thing: "Baby buggy for Mimi," she whispered. Mimi was her doll. How much did baby buggies cost? Jim didn't know.

Finally, Jim saw the lights of the town up ahead. There were at least two more miles to go, but he seemed to walk faster, knowing that his goal was near.

Mr. Hillman owned the store in Freeport. Every week, he gave Jim a list of items that would be on sale, starting Wednesday. Jim would paint the paper signs, and on Wednesday morning, the signs would appear on the front windows of Hillman's Grocery.

Actually, the grocery was more like an old-fashioned general store, because Hillman carried items other than foods. Now, during the approaching Christmas season, he had a few toys and decorations as well.

"Hello there, Jim. Wasn't sure you could make it in this storm. Have a seat by the stove, and I'll get you a cup of coffee," Hillman said.

Jim held the mug of coffee in his nearly frozen hands, savoring the warmth it provided. He looked around the store, and was surprised to see, on the top shelf, a small, yellow wicker doll carriage. Actually, just the right size for a little two-year-old girl to push.

"How much for the doll buggy on the shelf?" he asked Hillman.

"Well, I could let you have it for $1.50," the grocer replied.

"It's a deal," Jim said. And it was. The grocer handed Jim $2.00 for the signs, and the sign painter gave it back to him; receiving 50 cents in change and a yellow wicker baby buggy for Dena and Mimi.

A MESSAGE
FROM CYBERSPACE

"**G**ood morning, Mrs. Boyd. I am Dr. Maria Travis. How can I help you today?" Sara Boyd never thought she would be consulting a spiritualist. But here she was. Two years after her husband Ted's death, she was still mourning his passing, and disturbed by a strange occurrence involving her home computer.

"Well, after my husband died, something strange began happening. Not every day—usually just over weekends. I turn off the computer every night, but when I go to check e-mails in the morning, the power already is on."

"Was your late husband an avid computer user?"

"Oh, yes. He really enjoyed gathering information, playing computer games, keeping in touch with friends—those kinds of things."

"I see. And do you often use the computer, Mrs. Boyd?"

"I do keep in touch with friends through e-mailing, but my interest and skill levels are limited. I don't play games or pay bills online."

"You know," Travis said, "the spirits are always with us, watching over us, and moving around in our orbit. We may not see them, but they are here. Have you kept your husband's e-mail address?"

"Yes. I meant to delete it, but haven't yet. I have my own address."

"Have you tried sending him an e-mail?"

"Well no, of course not. How would I even do that?"

"Don't dismiss the idea. You could use your e-mail address. On the subject line write 'miss you,' or something like that, and then send a message."

"I never would have thought of doing that," Sara said.

"I suggest that you try it, and at our meeting next week, we can talk more about it."

For the first time in months, Sara felt encouraged that an answer to the computer puzzle might be simpler than she thought.

Every night before going to bed, Sara sent a message to Ted. But after a week, there were no responses.

Sara expressed her disappointment to Dr. Travis at their next session.

"I am not surprised," Travis said. If you have any doubt that this e-mailing will work, it won't. It is all about faith. You must have faith. You can also light some candles and burn incense while reciting the mantras I can provide."

Several weeks passed with no results, despite religiously lighting candles, burning incense, and reciting mantras. Sara realized that these sessions with Dr. Travis were costing her a bundle, too, so she cancelled her appointments.

Then, several days later, a message appeared in Sara's e-mail: *Nice going, Sara. Save your money. I'm saving a place for you. Love, Ted.*

RUNNING OUT OF STEAM

The apartment had that empty feeling, although it was filled with stacks of boxes, taped and labeled with their contents: dishware, china, silver, linens, and blankets.

Furniture was separated—most pieces marked for an estate sale; some better pieces ready to be shipped from Kansas to Ohio, along with the cartons.

A stylish wardrobe had been given today to Mrs. Dobson, the cleaning lady, who was grateful to have such splendid outfits.

My husband and I had reservations at a nearby inn. Movers were coming tomorrow.

Leda, David's 89-year-old mother, fell in her apartment and for the past two weeks lay languishing in the hospital, barely aware of her surroundings, and according to the doctor, hovering near death. "Just run out of steam," was the way he put it.

David really needed to get back to work, but we would wait another day or two.

The next day at the hospital, we were amazed to find Leda sitting up in a chair, eating her breakfast.

"I'm doing so much better today. In fact, the doctor says that I can probably go home in a few days," Leda said.

Never one to beat around the bush, David came right to the point. "Mother," he began, "you can't go back to living alone in a second floor walk-up. We will have to find a safe place for you."

Leda's face dropped as reality sank in.

"You are welcome to come and live with us," I volunteered.

But no, Leda wouldn't hear of it. "Leave all my friends, my bridge club, my church?" she said. "No, if there's a room at the Golden Ages Retirement Home, that's where I want to go."

That afternoon David and I visited the retirement home. The director showed us a nicely furnished room that would be available in three days.

Leda seemed relieved to know that we had found a room for her at the upscale retirement home. Oddly, she never asked about her furniture, crystal, china, or silver.

"I will need all my clothes, of course," Leda said. "They are hanging in garment bags in my bedroom closet. You can take them to my new place before you go back to Ohio."

We were so unprepared for this. I couldn't even look at David, who seemed to be saying, "All right, Mother."

In fact, it was anything but all right. We had given all the clothes to the cleaning lady.

That evening, after several telephone calls, we were finally able to reach Mrs. Dobson to explain the situation. And in an exchange that resembled a Secret Service covert operation, we met late that night at an abandoned gas station, where we transferred the garment bags from Dobson's truck to the back seat of our car.

All was well. I think, though, that at this point David and I were the ones running out of steam.

And, by the way, Leda continued to thrive at Golden Ages Retirement home for another ten years.

HEADS UP

Time for a haircut. I headed to my favorite *walk-ins welcome* salon. Two people ahead of me. Not bad.

"Next." The man stood up.

I took the chair beside the woman.

"Can you believe it?" she said. "I'm retired, and I'm still anxious."

"Maybe you worked too long?" I replied

"Are you kidding me? I loved my job."

"Oh"

"It's the service—terrible."

"Well, I like the service—never have to wait long for a haircut."

"Are you kidding me? I'm not talking about this salon."

"Oh"

"I'm talking about services at my house—getting a plumber, electrician, telephone guy—like that."

"Oh."

"I moved here from California. We had great services there."

"Maybe you want to move back to California?"
"Are you kidding me? Arizona's a great place to live."
"Oh."
"Next." The stylist motioned for the woman.
Thank God! She wasn't kidding.

THE IRISH RELATIVES

I remember when they arrived, as though it were yesterday; summer of 1947—the four of them, trudging along single file up Pine Street. The woman led the way. She wore a wrinkled blue print dress, stained under the arms on this muggy afternoon. Her dark hair was slipping out of its now messy up do. The battered suitcase she carried seemed to be weighing her down.

Behind her was a boy about seven or eight, carrying a smaller suitcase. Following him were two little girls I thought were twins; each clutching a stuffed animal.

The woman stopped in front of my house, where I sat on the porch sipping a glass of ice water.

"Which house is the Donovan's?" she asked.

I told her it was the next one, and that is where the four of them went.

Lily Donovan came to the door. I couldn't hear all of what was said, but *cousins from Ireland* was part of it.

When Mom came home from work, I told her about the visitors, and soon after, Mrs. Donovan came over to tell us about her guests, the Ryans from Ireland.

"Distant ones, I think," she said. "That would be from my mother's side of the family; that is, the Dunns from County Cork. Fiona says she is a friend of my second cousin, Mary Alice. Anyway, since our girls are off and married, we do have the spare bedroom with beds for the little girls, Jean and Sheila. The boy, Sean, can sleep on the closed-in porch. I just don't have a bed for cousin Fiona."

Mother told Mrs. Donovan that we had a roll-away bed she'd be glad to lend. Dad and Mr. Donovan could move it over after supper that night.

"Will the cousins be staying long?" Mother asked.

"The thing is," Mrs. Donovan said, "Fiona wants to move here. I told her she can stay until she finds a job and an apartment. Poor thing, I don't think she has much money. She told me her husband, Mike, was killed in the war. In Ireland, she worked in a pub. But, you know, she's family, and we'll do what we can for her."

I think my mother rolled her eyes on that one, knowing that the Donovans might have company for a long time.

And that is exactly what happened. Mrs. Donovan herself discouraged Fiona from seeking a job right away. The long boat trip to New York, and the bus trip to our town being so tiring and all.

Eventually, Fiona did check out the classifieds in the paper and circled a few possible places to apply for work. A Woolworths, White Tower Café, and a Lerner's Dress Shop—all on Main Street in the city nearby and on the bus route. But Fiona seemed to lack the qualifications for any of those jobs.

Then, it was almost time for school to begin. Fiona enrolled Sean in the local elementary school. Jean and Sheila were four years old, and would stay home. Sean needed school clothing, and because Fiona's money was running out, the Donovans bought clothes for him.

When Fiona began working at the local market, Mrs. Donovan became the main child care provider.

"Maybe you could supplement your salary by doing some sewing or babysitting," Mrs. Donovan suggested to Fiona. But Fiona didn't seem too keen about the ideas.

Frankly, the Donovans were becoming a bit tired of hosting their cousins from the old sod. In fact, Lily Donovan had written to her cousin, Mary Alice, several weeks ago about them.

Finally, a letter arrived from Mary Alice, who had moved and now lived in another town in Ireland. The letter from cousin Lily had been forwarded. As it turned out, Mary Alice said that she barely knew the Ryans. They actually were not related, she said. Also, Fiona's husband, Mike, wasn't killed in the war. "He is very much alive," reported Mary Alice, "and owner of a pub in Cork. I have told him of his family's whereabouts. You can expect to see him any day now, as he will be coming to claim his family. That Fiona—such a mess. Took money from the pub's till and took off without a word! Best if you don't mention this letter to Fiona, of course."

The red-haired Michael Ryan did arrive soon afterward, when he gathered up his brood and took them home.

Our roll-away bed went straight back to our spare room that very day.

SNOW DATE

S now had been falling all day, gently at first, now with more intensity, drifting across the rural highway, hampering visibility. When Jeff left the city, the storm had seemed moderate; the tall buildings served as barriers against the wind; the bright lights added warmth and security. Jeff was creeping along now, headlights on high beam, wipers going full tilt.

No plows or salt trucks had been on this road, Jeff was sure, as he struggled to keep the car from sliding into a ditch. He was already fifteen minutes late for a date with a young woman his sister, Joyce, had recently introduced him to at a fundraiser for the Humane Society.

Leslie had been Joyce's college roommate. Leslie's parents lived in the city, where her father was a well-known surgeon. But after graduation, she rented a small house in the country where she lived alone, working part-time for a veterinarian and teaching horseback riding.

Jeff thought her lifestyle was challenging, especially for a girl born and reared in the city. She seemed like a nice person, but the truth was, he wanted his sister to stop nagging him about being a bachelor. Anything to get her off his case. One date, it wouldn't kill him.

An invitation to dinner and a movie followed the meeting at the fundraiser. Now, Jeff hoped that he could find the turnoff to Leslie's house. At any rate, he'd reached the point of no return, since he certainly was closer to her house than to the city.

Suddenly, he saw someone by the side of the road, holding a lantern. At first, he didn't recognize Leslie, bundled up in a hooded jacket. He rolled down the window as she came up to the car. "Sorry I'm late," he laughed.

"I didn't know if you'd make it or not, but I didn't want you to end up in a ditch on this dark road. My phone's been out for three hours, or I would have called and told you not to come. Follow me, I've got a truck."

With a blade on the front of her truck, Leslie had cleared one narrow lane back to her small house.

A golden retriever named Sam bounded out when the front door opened, greeting Jeff like a long lost friend. A cheery fire crackled in the fireplace, and the room was filled with pleasant aromas from the kitchen.

Two places had been set on a small table by the fireplace. "I hope you like chicken stew and dumplings, Jeff. I'm not much of a cook, but this is the specialty of the house," Leslie said.

"Delicious," Jeff said, adding, "No apologies needed here."

Jeff and Leslie found that they knew many of the same people, although they had gone to different schools. They talked for quite a while.

"I'll help you with the dishes, and after that, I'd better get started for home," Jeff said.

But, Leslie discouraged that plan after looking out the window. "The trailer parked by the fence is empty; it has a heater and a bed. You're welcome to use it. By tomorrow, the plows will be through and you can go home in daylight—much safer that way."

Jeff hesitated, but decided to accept Leslie's offer. By this time, the snow was several inches deep, and the wind was blowing fiercely. Jeff could barely see the outline of the trailer.

Leslie pulled on high boots and a parka, grabbed the lantern, and led Jeff to the trailer where she turned on the heater and put sheets and blankets on the bed.

"See you in the morning," she said. Soon the trailer was warm, and Jeff quickly fell asleep.

Sunlight was streaming in the window when he heard a knock at the door. "Time to get up, city boy," Leslie called. "We have shopping to do. You'll find old clothes, jacket and boots in the closet by the kitchen."

By the time Jeff got suited up and opened the door, he saw Leslie on the roof of her small house, brushing off snow. She waved, and soon slid down into the snow and was leading him to the barn.

"What's going on?" he asked.

"We have to saddle up the horses and go down to the general store to get food for breakfast," she said.

Jeff didn't want to admit it, but he hadn't been on a horse in years. The idea of riding to the store in the snow wouldn't have occurred to him, but somehow, Leslie made it seem like the most natural thing in the world. His mount was a bay quarter horse named Willie, and Leslie was riding Jack, a chestnut Morgan.

Before long, Jeff's apprehension about the venture disappeared, and he and Leslie were laughing and talking as they had the previous evening.

The groceries were packed in saddle bags, and back at the house, Leslie cooked breakfast while she and Jeff listened to weather reports on the radio. Twelve inches of snow had fallen around the city, and the road department was working as quickly as possible to clear the highways.

By noon, the sun was shining and some melting had taken place. Plows came through and cleared the road in front of Leslie's house.

Jeff regretted that the time to leave had come. He thanked Leslie for her hospitality, and invited her out to dinner the next Friday.

The next week seemed to drag as Jeff waited for Friday. Fortunately, the weather was much improved, and driving to Leslie's house was easy.

"I've been looking forward to seeing you all week," Leslie said when she opened the door.

No pretentions here, Jeff thought. "Ditto, except that I was hoping for more snow and another sleep-over invitation," he laughed.

"Be careful what you wish for. Some sleepovers can end badly, like having to muck out horse stalls and such," Leslie quipped.

The evening was off to a good start, as Leslie and Jeff joked easily with each other, and were developing a warm friendship. They decided to have dinner at a Chinese restaurant after an early movie.

"What does your fortune cookie say?" Leslie asked.

"It says that I will be mucking horse stalls in the future," Jeff said. "Read me yours."

"Beware of handsome stall muckers," Leslie answered.

The two agreed to meet in town the next Saturday afternoon for an early dinner and a movie.

On the way to the restaurant where they were to meet, Jeff passed a jewelry store. He looked in the window, and was surprised to see Leslie with a man. She was trying on rings. The man Jeff recognized was the veterinarian for whom Leslie worked.

Jeff felt his hopes for a chance with Leslie diminishing. They had agreed to meet at six o'clock at the restaurant. Jeff was early, and selected the table. When Leslie arrived, he could see that she was in a happy mood. "Hi, Jeff. I've got some wonderful news to tell you," she said. "Order me a glass of white wine, and I'll tell you all about it."

Jeff ordered the wine, and felt his heart pounding as he waited to hear Leslie's news. He was sure it was the end of any plans he might have with Leslie.

The wine arrived, and Leslie lifted her glass. "My boss, Dr. Miller, is getting married to his high school sweetheart. Today, I helped him pick out an engagement ring. I am so happy for them," Leslie said. "Can I count on you to be my date for the June 10th wedding?"

"I'll have to check my calendar, but I think that will be okay," Jeff replied.

THEY PLAYED CHRISTMAS

Accordingto Helen, she must have had an angel watching over her; otherwise she wouldn't have survived the grim circumstances of her youth or been able to make the right choices that led to a better life. Now I hoped that an angel were there for me so I could do justice to her courageous story.

I was writing features for a small weekly newspaper in Kentucky. One day, my editor called me into his office promising a great story idea for me. He explained that it could even become a series of stories, with the focus being on people who had overcome difficulties and achieved success in later years.

A subscriber had come up with the idea, he said, because she was fed up with reading depressing news stories. She had even provided a list of people who had heroic stories to tell.

Helen's name was at the top of the list, and I was anxious to get started on the first story.

Located in the suburbs, Helen's house was a new townhouse furnished with a mixture of contemporary and antique furniture, colorful accents, and walls of family photos and paintings with pastoral themes.

A small, grey-haired woman I guessed to be in her mid-seventies greeted me at the door. Her blue eyes sparkled with good humor, and there was an appealing openness about her manner. We sat at a table in Helen's spacious kitchen, by a window with a view of the small patio garden.

"Before we start, let's have a little snack," Helen suggested. She filled two dishes with strawberry ice cream, and added a plate of chocolate cookies. I immediately felt at home, and I soon learned that being hospitable had been part of Helen's life from an early age.

Helen was raised on a small farm where tobacco, corn, and vegetables were grown. She was three years old at the height of the Great Depression when her mother died, prior to giving birth to a 14th child. The full-term, stillborn baby was delivered by caesarean, and placed in the casket at the mother's feet.

The official cause of the mother's death was flu, but I wondered: 14 pregnancies?

The survivors were seven girls and six boys, plus a stepson from the father's first marriage. Helen had a younger brother, Ben, who was 15 months old when their mother died.

There was no running water or electricity in that small farmhouse where the children slept three or four to a bed on well-worn mattresses.

Helen's special project was her baby brother, Ben. They were playmates and best friends, and when one by one the older siblings left home in their teens, she was more than ever like a mother to him at a very young age, doing most of the day to day household chores as well.

There were no presents at Christmas, but that didn't stop Helen and Ben from playing Christmas. It was a game, you see. The game could take place any time of the year, but more often, it happened when the weather became cooler—maybe even after the first frost.

The two children would go out on the country road and cut tiny cedar trees that they brought home and decorated with paper chains. "I remember being so excited," Helen said.

Birthdays were celebrated with the father administering a series of whacks on the posterior in accordance with the number of birthdays being observed.

Life on the farm was not easy. Drinking water came from a well, but in summer, they would go to a farm some four or five miles away and get barrels of water for the tobacco and vegetable plants. They got up at three or four o'clock in the morning to work in the fields before the afternoon heat arrived.

"Our father ordinarily did not cook, but in the fall, he would make a huge pot of soup from the last of the vegetables. We canned foods when we got home from school, staying up most of the night and then going to school as usual the next day," Helen remembered.

Hogs were killed in November. Sausage was cold-packed, put into jars, and grease was poured over them before sealing.

Although the father didn't make a habit of celebrating most holidays, he observed one Memorial Day tradition, which was somewhat unusual. He would place a long string in the yard, gather flowers, and make them into small bouquets, line them up on the string, and cut the string to tie up each bunch. Then, the children loaded them in a little red wagon, took them to the cemetery, and placed them on graves.

The nearest neighbors were the Culps—Dorothea and Roland, who lived in a big house about five miles east. Mr. Culp was the proprietor of a farm equipment company, and he owned property in the area. After he died of a heart attack, his widow remained in the house, and once a month collected rents from tenants in a nearby town.

"I remember how prim and proper I thought Mrs. Culp was," Helen said. "She drove a nice car, and she always dressed well."

Sometimes, Mrs. Culp would invite Helen and Ben to ride with her to the town when she collected rents. Sitting ramrod straight in the front seat, with Helen and Ben in back, Mrs. Culp would ask them about school, and comment on various local events.

After making several stops to collect rents, Helen and Ben noticed that Mrs. Culp's driving skills on the way home were somewhat diminished, as she kept swerving onto the berm.

"We thought she had eye problems. Ben and I muffled giggles at the absurdity of the situation, but we feared for our lives just the same.

"As an adult, I wondered if some of the renters plied their landlord with a touch of the grape—particularly if they were short of cash that month," Helen said.

Occasionally, Mrs. Culp asked Helen and her sister, Pat, to help clean out her basement. The pay might be five cents or a stick of gum, plus some canned goods she had stored.

"The cans always were rusted, but we took them and ate the contents, remarkably without getting sick," Helen remembered.

On the other side of Helen's house, also some five miles away, there lived the Merrill family—seven children and their parents. Mr. Merrill was a minister in a Pentecostal church.

Helen said, "He never preached to us, or tried to convert us, but he was always ready to help when help was needed. He had a wagon, and would take our rain barrel to the pond to be filled. He let us pick strawberries on his property. I often think about what nice people the Merrills were, even though they couldn't have approved of my father's lifestyle."

Helen found her own way to God and to the Baptist Church where she was baptized at age 12. No one in the family came to witness the event.

A strong faith in God and the healing power of prayer would sustain Helen then and in all the years ahead. Nobody in her family went to church. In later years, she heard a story that her father had once attended a service dressed in his bib overalls, and ended up becoming the object of ridicule from the pulpit because of his attire. That was the last time he had ever gone to church, so far as Helen knew.

As soon as she was old enough to apply for a work permit, Helen got a part-time job as a nurse's aide at a nearby hospital. She worked after school every day for a small amount of money while continuing to do most of the work around the house at home.

As a young teenager, Helen became increasingly aware of a situation in the home which she found unpleasant as well as frightening.

Her father was a drinker, and frequently, men would come to the house and drink with him. The idea of getting away from this permanently was a constant, nagging thought. But, there always was the belief that Ben needed her and she couldn't leave him.

Then the time came when leaving not only was the best thing to do, but the only thing that made sense.

One Saturday, Helen's father said, "You stay home and clean the house today."

By noon, Helen had the place spic and span. The laundry and other chores around the house were done. "I thought, I might as well go to work, surely he won't mind my earning a little money."

So Helen took the bus to the hospital and worked the afternoon shift.

When the father came home later that day and found out where she was, he was irate. He went to the hospital, and made Helen walk the 10 miles back home. That was the punishment for disobeying. Well, that was part of it. The rest was something Helen would rather forget.

A severe beating was the rest of it—painful blows to the chest and stomach. After that, Helen's resolve was firm. She would leave. Her moment mercifully had arrived.

The departure had to be timed right, though. It had to be when her father was away from home. On the day selected, she made sure all the household chores were done, and Ben knew what to fix for supper.

Helen gathered her few belongings and got ready to meet the three o'clock bus at the end of the road.

"Oh no! Where are my shoes? Ben, have you seen my shoes?"

she cried. She looked everywhere—under beds, in closets, every room in the house, and even on the porch. There were no shoes anywhere. Ten minutes to three. "I've got to have the shoes. Ben, help me look." And, he pretended to do just that.

"I think they're gone forever," he said. "Guess you can't leave," he added.

Five minutes to go, and Helen had a suspicion that Ben knew where the shoes were. "Please, Ben, I need those shoes. Do you have them?"

And, at the last possible moment, a shamefaced Ben handed over the shoes. Helen practically ran to meet the bus. The guardian angel prevailed. The bus, for the first time, was a few minutes late.

Helen breathed a sigh of relief as she sat down by a window on the bus. She said a little prayer as well, to thank God for helping her.

She had decided to go to a small community some 20 miles away, where an older sister, Leah, and her husband, Ray, operated a general store. Fearing that if anyone found out about her plan it never would have gotten off the ground, Helen told no one—not even her sister.

Years later, Helen would remember the bus ride to her sister's as the longest 20 miles she ever had traveled.

Leah was straightening up some shelves when Helen walked into the store. "Well, this is a nice surprise," she said, dropping a sack of flour on the floor, and hurrying over to give Helen a welcoming hug. "I can't imagine how you got away on a Saturday, but I'm glad to see you."

The tears Helen had held back for so long came pouring out. "Oh, sis, I've gone for good. I'm never going back to live in that house. Will you help me?"

Without hesitation, Leah assured her that going back home wasn't an option. "Of course I'll help you, and Ray will too. We don't know how you've stood it this long."

And, for the first time that she could recall, Helen felt that someone really cared about what happened to her. It was a good feeling.

But after supper that night, an older brother, Don, came to the door. "Get your things, Helen. Time to go home. Dad's furious, so be prepared for a big blowup."

Leah stood between Don and Helen. "She's not going anywhere, and that's final. Her days in that awful place are over, and Dad's fury doesn't scare us. What scares us is his drinking and his drinking friends—so, get lost. Ray and I will take care of things from now on."

And that was that.

On Monday morning, Leah and Helen went to the hospital where Leah asked to see the administrator. Sitting in his office, Leah pleaded Helen's case, asking him to let her young sister stay at the nurse's quarters while continuing to work after school and on weekends.

Mr. Ellis was a kind man who knew about Helen's home situation, and who also recognized that she had been a dependable employee as well as an excellent worker during the past couple of years.

"I think we can help you," Ellis said, adding, "Helen can have a bed in the dormitory, and take her meals with the other girls. If $3.00 a week suits you, it's a deal."

The next stop was the high school, some 10 miles away. The principal listened to Leah's explanation of Helen's change in residency, and offered a suggestion of his own. "I live a few blocks from the hospital, and Helen can ride with me to school and back."

So it was settled. Helen lived at the nurse's quarters for her last two years in high school, and she was able to work a few more hours each week at the hospital, including weekends and holidays. There was no doubt in her mind that nursing would be her career choice. She felt at home in the environment, and she seemed to have a talent for helping the sick.

Occasionally, she visited her father and Ben—even did what she could around the house while there, preparing supper or cleaning. Although the reception was a bit cool, there was no talk of her returning on a permanent basis.

As it happened with her baptism, no one came to her graduation from high school. Of course, there were no gifts either. "I remember the night of graduation, watching families and friends of many graduates coming to the school and bringing presents. I thought how nice that was, but really, I didn't resent the fact that none of them were for me. I guess that would seem strange to a lot of people," Helen said.

After graduation, Helen worked full-time at the hospital and continued to live at the nurse's home. It would be a long, slow process, but she was saving money to pay for nursing school.

It wasn't all work, of course. On weekends, the nurses whose shifts would permit, hosted parties in the recreation room. They danced to music provided by records on an old Victrola, or gathered around the upright piano to sing popular songs. On these occasions, young men from the local college joined them.

Helen hadn't known much of a social life, and in those days, was quite shy. However, she looked forward to being part of the get-togethers.

One young man, Will Richard, was especially nice to Helen. He found her shyness refreshing compared to the more forward co-eds at his college.

Will came from a prominent family in the college town where they lived. When Helen realized this, she believed that her chances for anything more than friendship were limited, and she focused even more on her plans to become a nurse.

But when Will invited her on a regular date, Helen couldn't say no. Kathryn, a nurse at the hospital, and Helen's roommate, was excited to hear the news. Since she and Helen were the same size, she insisted that her friend wear one of her own favorite blue dresses.

Will drove up in his new 1951 Buick that Saturday night to take Helen to a movie. Despite the differences in their backgrounds, conversation came easily. They had similar interests, liked the same kinds of music, and laughed often.

A few more dates followed, one memorable goodnight kiss, and then came the nasty telephone call. Helen never was sure who the caller was, although the message was plain enough. "Stay away from Will Richard, or you'll be very sorry. This not a joke," the female voice warned.

Helen assumed that Will had received a warning too, because the invitations stopped. In fact, he rarely came to the weekend parties after that. When he did, his manner was reserved. The situation wasn't discussed, and Helen believed that Will had lost interest.

That was okay with her; she didn't question it. After all, Helen had learned early in life to accept disappointment.

When there was a phone call for her several weeks later, it was Will, acting as though no time had elapsed, and asking Helen to a dance at his college. Helen didn't hesitate to accept.

The dance was a new beginning for Will and Helen. Their romance blossomed.

After Will graduated from college, he took a position in a local department store while Helen continued her work at the hospital, and began her studies there to become a registered nurse.

Will joined the National Guard and took four months off from work to attend Officer's Candidate School in Oklahoma.

There were frequent telephone calls, and many letters, and after a couple of months, Will invited Helen to visit him. Spring break was coming up, and Helen agreed to make the trip to Oklahoma.

Then, a few days before the scheduled train trip, Will called. "I've been thinking, if we can find a place to live out here, we can get married," he casually announced.

Helen tried to contain her excitement over this unorthodox and unexpected proposal. "Oh, okay," she said, hoping her nervousness wasn't detected.

The next day, she had the required blood test, bought a new dress—a wedding dress—in case she and Will could find a place to live. Helen knew she would be putting her dream of becoming a nurse on hold, but she never doubted that it would happen someday.

The train trip was long and tiring, and Helen arrived at the station in Oklahoma early in the morning. There was no one to meet her. Will was on duty, so Helen walked to the hotel where a room for her had been reserved.

Later that day, Helen met Will in the hotel lobby. They had coffee in a small restaurant nearby, and talked about the wedding. It was decided that they could look for an apartment later, since the hotel reservation was for a week—plenty of time to look for housing, they thought.

They found a minister who agreed to marry them the next night, Saturday, at 7:00 p.m.

Will was on duty until 4:00 p.m. that day. With time to spare before the wedding, the two went looking for a place to eat, ending up at the bus station. The fare they chose became a tradition for future anniversary celebrations: pimiento cheese sandwiches and cokes.

After the wedding, the couple spent the evening at the officer's club on base, where for a few hours, no one knew they were married. When the news came out, nobody could understand why they chose to spend all that time at the club.

The next week, Helen went to the Red Cross, where information about housing for the military was available. "The room was filled with young women. We each took a number, and when ours was called, we were interviewed. The woman next to me got tired of waiting, and handed me her number. She no sooner left than that number was called," Helen remembered.

The best prospect was three rooms in a private home where they would share a bathroom with other members of the family. It would have to do—in fact, the young couple thought their choice was a pretty good one.

After the officer's training session was over, Will and Helen returned to their hometown. He went back to his job at the store, and Helen continued working at the hospital and studying for her R.N.

When the state board examinations were to be given in the city

35 miles away, Helen was eight months pregnant. Her doctor told her, "Of course, you can't go." But, Helen knew that if she didn't go then, she never would. So, when the bus pulled up to the hospital and the other women boarded, Helen was there with them.

To be eligible for certification, candidates took tests over a period of three days. They stayed at a hotel near the examination center. It so happened that a representative from a maternity clothing company was also staying at the hotel. He came up to Helen and asked her if she would model one of the dresses in his collection. She agreed to do that, and for her efforts, received as a gift, the pretty outfit she wore.

All's well that ends well. Helen passed her state boards with flying colors, received her certification, and one month later, the Richard's first child was born.

The Richard's second child, a son also, was born four years later on his brother's birthday.

In many ways, it seemed that Helen and Will led a charmed life, but as with all couples, there were ups and downs—good times, not so good times, and much later—tragedy.

And, Helen found a friend in her loving mother-in-law, who may have had some doubts about her son's marriage in the beginning, but soon welcomed her daughter-in-law into the family. In fact, Mrs. Richard made the first birthday cake Helen ever had.

Helen and Will spent every Christmas day with his family. Not all those events were picture perfect. The Christmas when Helen was six months pregnant with the second child, the men in the family locked themselves in a bedroom where son, Tommy, was sleeping. When he awakened, they made him go out the window and come around to the front door. The little boy had a cold, and wasn't dressed for the weather.

Helen was furious when she found out what had happened. She confronted her husband and, finding a glass of water conveniently at hand, poured the entire contents over his head.

"Don't you ever do that again," he admonished.

"I will if I want to," was Helen's reply.

Helen's childhood memories of Christmases with the only gifts being a box of fruit and canned goods from her older sister's general store, and no personal gifts, kept the Richards from going overboard. This surprised Will's sisters, who lavished their own children with toys, while Tommy and baby Paul each received only one toy.

There were many relocations to other states through Will's work; some 18 in all, and usually the business of moving fell to Helen. Helen remembered putting a 'for sale' sign in the yard one Sunday morning. A neighbor family saw the sign as they left for church, and when they returned, the sign was gone.

On Paul's first birthday, he awakened that morning uttering a strange cry. He was running a high fever, and Helen called the doctor, who advised giving Paul baby aspirin. The fever went down, but later, when Helen was feeding him some of the birthday cake she had made, little Paul suffered a convulsion. He was rushed to the hospital where some tests, including a brain scan, were given. The doctor suspected epilepsy, but the tests, he said, didn't indicate it.

The child was kept at the hospital overnight, and while Helen sat at his bedside, he suffered another convulsion. The doctor diagnosed his condition as being a nervous disorder, and prescribed medicine he was to take until he was four years old.

Later though, as an adult, Paul had seizures, and was given medication to control them as well as medication for bi-polar illness.

Paul grew up to become an accomplished musician and songwriter. He married, and he and his wife had a child. The marriage was troubled and the couple separated. They were in the process of working out their differences when suddenly, at the home of friends, Paul died after suffering a grand mal seizure. He was 45 years old.

Helen and Will were shocked and devastated by their younger son's death. "It was a terrible year," Helen said, adding, "In many ways, it was harder for Will and my mother-in-law. The kids growing up in my family weren't permitted to cry. I felt that I had to be the strong one, even though my heart was breaking too."

These days, grandson Tom, now an adult and so very like his father in appearance and sweet temperament, is a frequent visitor. "Sometimes we forget, and call him Paul," Helen said.

Son Tom lives less than 100 miles away, and has written several novels.

As a way of dealing with the tragedy in their lives, Helen and Will have become more involved in volunteer work at a local mission, usually including serving Christmas dinner, delivering meals on wheels, and taking elderly people to doctor's appointments.

That's a wrap, I foolishly thought as I turned in my copy of the first story on my to-do list.

"Not so fast," said the editor when he called the next day after reading it. "This story cries out for more. I want to read more," he said, adding, "Whatever happened to the head nurse at that hospital? Apparently she was helpful to Helen. Is she still living? If so, can you interview her? Get going."

I was torn between thinking my editor was nit-picking, and feeling a little ashamed that I hadn't thought of his idea of adding more to the story. When my ego was under better control, I called Helen.

"I heard that Jean Taylor still is alive, in her eighties and living near the hospital in a nursing home," Helen said. She promised to find out the name of the home and call me the next day.

A few days later, I drove to the small town where Miss Taylor lived, and was surprised to find her sitting in her room and willing to be interviewed.

"I certainly remember Helen," Taylor said. "She came from a very sad home, but she was bright and eager to work, and she deserved a chance to improve her life. All of us at the hospital were glad to help her do that. Of course, it was all worthwhile because her life turned out so well. We were all proud of her."

"Was there a special reason why you were so willing to help her," I asked. She hesitated for a few minutes before answering.

"I grew up in a loving family—at least, it was so long as everything went along smoothly, and nobody committed any glaring mistakes. My older sister, Jenny, made the mistake of becoming pregnant when she was 15 years old, and the worst part was that she had been raped by someone in the community.

"Jenny never told anyone about the rape, and when her condition became apparent, she refused to reveal the name of the father.

"Of course, rape was never discussed. In those days, most people blamed the woman. My parents were completely unsupportive. They kicked Jenny out of the house. Can you guess where she ended up? The priest at the Episcopal Church took her in, and she helped the housekeeper with some of the chores around the house. When the time came for the birth, it was the priest who took her to the hospital.

"Naturally, many people in the town assumed at first that the priest, Father Michael, was the baby's father. The vestry, in fact, was ready to have him deposed, but the housekeeper, Fanny Ellison, went to the vestry meeting, and told the members that the father was a young man, formerly of the parish, who had left the community. She said that all of them would be shocked if she told them his name."

Miss Taylor said that the baby was an adorable little girl, and Jenny named her Robyn. Mrs. Ellison offered Jenny a room in her home. Jenny was able to finish her high school education, and found a job in a clothing store. She worked hard, saved as much money as she could, and when Robyn was four years old, they rented a small house in a rural area, which Jenny thought would be the ideal place for raising a child.

The elementary school where Robyn would attend was a short walk for their house. There was plenty of room to play, and there were many children the same age as Robyn in the neighborhood.

Jenny delighted in watching Robyn grow. Her sweet personality and winning smile kept up Jenny's spirits. Her only regret was that because her parents still would have nothing to do with her, they were missing out on the joy of being grandparents.

But, sometimes, miracles do happen, and one Sunday afternoon, a few days before Robyn's fifth birthday, Jenny's parents came to visit, and met their little grandchild for the first time. Surprisingly, the meeting was pleasant, though somewhat formal, and there was hope for future get-togethers.

The Taylors brought with them some gifts for Robyn: toys, and a yellow raincoat, hat, and matching boots.

"You'll need these when you go to school," Mrs. Taylor said, and she obviously was pleased when Robyn showed appreciation for the gifts, and immediately donned the rain outfit.

"The day school started, it was raining, and Robyn was glad that she could wear her new rain gear," Jean Taylor remembered.

At this point in the story, Ms. Taylor's eyes filled with tears, and she paused for a few seconds before continuing.

"As the little group of children neared the school where the crossing guard held out a sign to stop traffic, a car came careening down the road, knocking little Robyn to the pavement. Two other little girls were hit, but their injuries were not fatal.

"Robyn died on the way to the hospital. The impact of the crash had been so severe that the new yellow rain boots flew off the child's feet, and were found several yards away by the side of the road.

"I hadn't been able to help my sister when our parents turned her out of their house many years ago, and left her to fend for herself. The tragic way in which her life turned out had a lot to do with my decision to become a nurse and to devote my life to helping people whenever possible. Helen was a case in point. She was a hard worker, a good person, and the victim of a bad home life; yet it wasn't in Helen to hold a grudge."

From Miss Taylor, I learned that Robert Williams, the school's retired principal, was living in a small nearby town. I decided to drive there, and talk to him, if possible.

Williams lived by himself in a small bungalow. Although confined to a wheelchair, he answered the doorbell on the first ring, and after giving my name, he said that a call from Miss Taylor had alerted him to my visit.

He had a keen memory of Helen, and was interested in the story I was writing. I was eager, I told him, to know if there was a particular reason why he had been willing to help Helen continue attending the high school where he was principal.

Williams closed his eyes for a few moments, as though gathering his thoughts, and trying to decide what to reveal of the past.

"I was very concerned about Helen's family situation, and about her future, which seemed bleak at best. I knew that she had great potential, and I wanted to do what I could to help," he said.

I sensed that there was more to the story, and asked him if anything in his life had influenced the way in which he reacted to Helen.

"There is a painful memory in my life that never strays far from the surface," he said. "It happened when I was a senior in high school. There was an attractive girl in my class who lived in an area considered to be on the wrong side of the tracks.

"My parents were kind of snobbish, and would have been opposed to my relationship with her. One night, after a dance at the school, I walked with her part of the way to her home, leaving her to go the rest of the way alone.

"The next day, I learned that she had been murdered before she reached home. The police questioned those who had been at the dance. I never volunteered that I had probably been the last person to see the girl alive. I feared my parents' reaction to my having been with her, and of being a possible suspect.

"As it was, several classmates had seen the two of us leaving together, and I became the number one suspect in her murder. I was questioned repeatedly by the police, but was finally let go for lack of evidence.

"The perpetrator never was found, but my reputation in that

town was ruined. The worst part though, was the shame I felt in having kept information from the police.

"I graduated from high school, went on to college, moved many miles away from my hometown, taught school, and eventually became a principal.

"I suppose that helping Helen was my way of trying to be a better person, atoning for my mistakes, and doing some good where it was needed."

On the way home, I thought about the people who had played a role in Helen's remarkable story.

In some way, all of them had played Christmas—from the children whose enthusiastic spirit made a tradition of gathering tiny cedar trees and decorating them with paper chains, to the adults who so willingly provided help when needed. May the game never end.

THE REMARKABLE
THREE-GAITED HORSE

Nora Bennett couldn't recall exactly when she first got the notion of entering the Darren County Fair's three-gaited, all breed horse competition the summer she turned 55. It was something she had thought about for a long time though—after her husband, Ned, had bought her the handsome, liver-chestnut Morgan for her 50th birthday.

In a way, it was strange—Nora's newly-acquired interest in horses. She hadn't grown up around them. The few times she had ridden as a young teenager hadn't been especially memorable, other than having sore muscles the next day.

Moving from Ohio to Tennessee, where horses were as common as cats and dogs, was at least partly responsible for stirring up an interest in equines. That, and her job as a reporter for a small, farm publication, where her varied duties included several assignments writing about people in the horse business, had led to taking riding lessons.

The lessons were provided by a local character from the old school, who had practically grown up on a horse, had trained horses and jockeys for the racetrack, and who claimed that two days before his birth, over eighty years ago, his mother, a noted horsewoman, had competed in a neighborhood race, and won.

When Nora arrived for her first lesson, offered in return for her help with some chores around the barn, Cal Thomas met her at the gate. He stood tall and erect, a slender man with curly, silvery hair, wearing coveralls and a broad-brimmed straw hat.

"Stop that, hush," he said sternly to a small black dog that was barking and running in circles around him, as though protecting his master from a threatening intruder. "He won't bother you, come right on in," Thomas reassured Nora. And immediately, all kinds of barnyard animals came charging out of the shed row—a couple of geese, a goat who jumped up on Nora, and a shivering, odd-looking white dog who looked as though he'd been put together backwards.

"That's Melvin. He was in some kind of terrible accident, left by the side of the road, and Doc rescued him. She got him fixed up and he's been with us ever since," Thomas said. Doc, as Nora found out, was Thomas' good friend and live-in companion—a veterinarian whose office was located on the farm.

"Come on over here, Mrs. Bennett," Thomas pointed in the direction of a bale of straw, covered with a saddle, "and we'll get started on your first lesson, after you put this on," he said, handing her a jockey's helmet.

"Where's the horse?" Nora asked, looking in every direction.

"In time, in time," Thomas replied. "The bale of straw is the first horse. You learn to sit properly, fall off left and right, post, handle the reins. Then put all of that knowledge together and avoid some mistakes and serious accidents when you finally sit on a live horse."

Thomas held the bridle, seated in front of the bale of straw, and barked orders like a marine sergeant.

Nora couldn't believe how sore she was after the first thirty minute lesson, but she was determined to learn the skill of riding.

Twice a week after that, she came to Thomas' barn for a lesson on the bale of straw.

In exchange for the lessons, Nora helped groom, bathe and hot walk horses, and learned the proper way to prepare a stall.

Nora's friends thought it was the biggest joke in the world to learn horseback riding on a bale of straw. "You can't be serious," Nora's tennis partner, Madge Raymond said, when she first heard about it. In fact, at every get-together, Nora's bale of straw was the topic of conversation.

Madge had learned to ride at the age of six—"right up on a real horse," she said—and without a wimpy helmet, either."

What put a stop to jokes about the bale of straw maneuver was a movie, "The Black Stallion," in which a horse trainer, played by Mickey Rooney, teaches a young charge how to ride: first putting him on an old bale of straw.

The big day finally arrived for Nora. The horse selected for her debut was a crossbred draft horse that stood 18.5 hands high, and wore a custom-made girth. Everything she'd learned on the bale of straw came in handy, although her first several riding experiences astride this giant horse took place in the confinement of the shed row, and involved riding from one end to the other and making sharp turns.

Eventually, Nora was riding three or four times a week, progressing from the shed row to the bridle path, and then to short and finally longer trail rides around the farm.

It was only a matter of time—less than a year—before Nora would be talking about getting a horse of her own. Mr. Thomas agreed to help in selecting the right kind of horse for Nora. But the ones she liked he thought were too expensive. The ones he liked "aren't very pretty," she told Ned, adding, "Naturally, they're cheap. We've been all over the county looking at horses, Ned. He haggles over price just like he does over the price of hay. When I finally asked him how much he thought I should pay for a horse, he said, 'not more than $350.' Shoot—what kind of horse could you expect to get for $350, an old nag?"

Still, the old man knew horses and could spot trouble a mile away. Once, when they went to see an Arabian beauty a man bragged about, saying he was selling because he'd fallen on hard times, Thomas looked him straight in the eye and asked, "How long has the horse been curbed?"

That, of course, marked the end of a brief visit.

The summer was nearly over, and Nora was getting impatient. She wanted a horse of her own, and was determined to find one, with or without Thomas' help. Then, she spotted an ad in the local newspaper. "For sale: Morgan gelding; 15 hands, gentle. Call 345-6297 for appointment."

Nora went to see the horse first by herself, then with Ned and Thomas. The horse was a beauty, and seemed gentle enough. The owner, a tall, young blond-haired woman, described him as "very typey," even though he had no papers. "It hardly matters though," she said, adding, "He's gelded."

Thomas wanted to see Nora ride the horse, whose name, unfortunately, was 'Satan' "You can always change his name, Mrs. Bennett," Thomas assured her, as he gave her a leg up. Nora took Satan through his paces—walk, trot, canter, in both directions. He appeared to be cooperative enough. Thomas didn't say a word until they'd left, after telling the owner they would be in touch.

Back in the car, Nora asked Thomas what he thought of the horse. "Well, I don't know," he replied, "How much is the woman asking?"

"Eight hundred, and she'll include the bridle and bit," Nora said.

"Whew!" Thomas said, and that was all.

Nora had promised Satan's owner an answer the next day. She talked on the phone with Thomas a few more times, expecting him to help her, but finally realized that the decision was up to her. In a moment of uncharacteristic impetuosity, Nora chose the horse.

The first thing Nora did after having Satan trailered to Thomas' farm where he would be boarded, was to change his name to 'Nate,' mostly because Nora was haunted by an old saw: never ride a horse named Devil; never eat at Mom's Restaurant, and never play cards with a man called Doc."

But changing Satan's name seemed to have the opposite effect from the one intended. Day after day, Nora would groom him, tack him up and mount, only to discover that he was more mule than horse. He simply refused to move.

"We'll bring him around," Thomas kept saying. But after a couple weeks of this kind of obstinate behavior, Thomas, who normally was patient, used a firmer tone of voice with the stubborn animal. He rode him a few times himself, and in another week, Nate at least would walk back and forth in the shed row.

It took a lot of tender loving care and patience to "bring the horse around." But Nate finally got back to doing his three gaits. On one occasion though, he took the bit in his mouth and raced at breakneck speed around the farm, finally stopping at the barn door where the manager stood, frantically waving his arms and yelling, "Whoa!"

It was an experience Nora never would forget. More than ever, she was convinced that Thomas had been right with his bale of straw teaching method.

"I'll say this for you, you've got a good seat on a horse," Nora's tennis-playing friend, Madge, commented after watching Nora take Nate through his paces. "You ought to enter the county fair horse show sometime," Madge suggested.

But four years passed before Nora had the courage to do that. Each year though, the fair board sent her an application, and the time came when Nora filled out the form, returned it with her $10 entry fee, and took a serious look at her riding clothes. She had the helmet, but the composition boots she'd been wearing were in bad shape. The event would require new boots.

"You might as well get what you need," Ned encouraged, suggesting that looking good was part of the competition.

A pair of black, English leather field boots, a white equestrian-style blouse and grey breeches were selected, as well as a new black velveteen cover for the Caliente helmet.

Hal Sammons, the barn manager, agreed to transport Nate to the fairgrounds and back to the stable after the show. Everything was set.

The one sad note, and it was a big one, was that Cal Thomas had died two weeks before, and Nora wasn't at all sure she could go through with her plans to compete. Sammons talked her into it. "He would have wanted you to, Mrs. Bennett; you know that," he encouraged.

The day of the horse show dawned bright and sunny. Too sunny, in fact, because the temperatures soared into the 90s, with high humidity as well. Several classes in the show were cancelled because participants failed to arrive.

This meant that the class Nora had signed up for came sooner than she expected—much too soon and before she had a chance to get Nate used to the ring.

The riders were told to enter the ring and walk their horses counter-clockwise. But this is where the trouble began. Nate took off at a gallop, and the controls Nora normally used failed. All she seemed able to do was to steer him around the other horses and avoid a major collision.

When the ringmaster called for a pause and "reverse directions," Nate obediently stopped, reversed and began galloping in the direction other horses were walking. The same thing happened during the calls for trot and canter.

Out of the corner of her eye, Nora, who really was concentrating on keeping her seat, could see Ned up in the bleachers, camera focused on her and Nate, as though what they were doing was the work of international champions, and worthy of being immortalized on film.

Finally, the nightmare was over. The contest was completed. It had lasted but a few minutes, although it seemed like a lifetime. Nora moved the by now exhausted horse over to the lineup where the judges were reviewing the entrants. Nate rose to the occasion, lifted his tail high, pointed his ears forward and stretched out—just like a pro.

Outside the ring, Nora dismounted, handed the reins to Ned, and went to the fair board office where she telephoned Hal Sammons. "Hi gal, how'd it go?" Sammons asked.

"Anybody wanna buy a horse?" Nora answered. They both laughed at that one—knowing that Nora wasn't about to sell Nate. The two had been through too much together, the middle-aged woman and the remarkable three-gaited horse. So what if the three gaits were merely variations of a gallop: fast, faster, fastest?

Nora could almost hear Mr. Thomas saying, "A good ride is when you come back still sitting in the saddle." That was one way to look at it.

A LIGHT LUNCH
FOR THE BISHOP

Entertaining the bishop of a large Midwestern diocese might not faze some people, but Ellen Holt was rendered nearly helpless by the awesome prospect. She could thank her good-natured husband, Jim, for the way it came about, actually. It was his fault for reading, in detail, every piece of literature that crossed his desk. This time, a particular church magazine article about an upcoming conference in the South piqued Jim Holt's curiosity. "It says here, that Dr. C. Charles Calvert Compton will be the main speaker at Sewanee. Did you know he's a bishop now?"

"You mentioned it once," Ellen said. But neither she nor Jim was surprised at Compton's success, recalling that as rector of an affluent Episcopal parish in Ohio, Dr. Compton, who married them 30 years ago, was an outstanding man, and a gifted speaker; definitely destined for greater things.

"I think I'll call him," Jim said, and although it was early in the day, Ellen knew that before long, a telephone call would be placed, and so it was. Her husband was a man of his word.

Dr. Compton, now Bishop Compton, couldn't actually remember having married the Holts, or baptizing one of their children three years after that, but it was nice to hear from Jim, the bishop said.

As it turned out, Bishop Compton and his wife, Susan, would be driving to the University of the South, and would be going through Campbellsburg. An invitation was issued on the spot, and the Comptons agreed to stop there for lunch with the Holts on a Tuesday, two weeks hence.

The rector and his wife, the Rev. John Stone and Marcia, from the Holts' present home church, St. Mary's, were invited too, so that a group of six would fill out the dining room table nicely, and the group gathered there would have some common basis for conversation.

It needs to be said though, at this point, that cooking was not Ellen Holt's strong suit. She could prepare food well enough, but her imagination was hardly a creative one, and her repertoire was limited. That is to say, she could assemble a passable meat loaf, a substantial beef stew, and a tasty enough tuna casserole. Gourmet cooking, however, was as foreign to her experience as it was to her palate.

Guests did not accept invitations to the Holts' home because of the fancy food. They came because the Holts made everyone feel welcome and tried to put good conversational groups together. Parties in their home were fun.

Still, Ellen Holt worked hard on the planning, and while plain, her menus were put together with an emphasis on good nutrition and ample servings. She would agonize for days over the menu for this particular lunch for the bishop.

The season was spring, so hot food wouldn't necessarily be required for the meal, but that knowledge was of little help. From casseroles to soups, salads, sandwiches, and desserts, Ellen pored over cookbooks and women's magazines until her eyes were red and her neck hurt.

Meanwhile, time was growing short and decisions had to be made. It was definitely the moment to call for help.

The helpers were four neighbors, close friends who always came to the rescue in times of trouble, and showed interest and enthusiasm as well, when celebrations were in order.

So it was that Ellen made four telephone calls the week before the luncheon, and asked her friends to come by for coffee and a brainstorming session.

Characteristically, Leslie, whose concept of entertaining was to have all social events catered, made the first suggestion. "Why not order in? Serve some sherry to start. When everybody raves about the food, take a bow, and never let on you didn't slave over a hot stove."

It wasn't a bad idea, and one Ellen actually might consider, if she could decide on a menu. The menu was the big problem. Carol came up with an even easier plan, tempting, but more expensive, too. "Take everybody out to a nice restaurant. You don't have to do a thing but smile. Just be sure to bring your plastic." That would take care of any menu concerns.

Dottie, who liked the idea of home entertainment, but hated to cook, and rejected ordering in, came up with another option. "Have somebody prepare and serve the food in your own home. It's friendlier, but you still can relax and enjoy your guests. I've got names of people you could contact."

But it was Jean Lund, finally, whose idea won out. Jean never failed to give good advice, along with a large helping of humor, and an understanding of Ellen's capabilities.

"You can do it yourself. Just make it simple, like vichyssoise, green salad, and crème fraiche, or quiche Lorraine and," Jean didn't quite finish her sentence before Ellen interrupted.

"Right. You know I make it a point never to prepare anything I can't spell, pronounce, or translate. It's got to be really simple, please," she pleaded.

"Okay then, how about peanut butter sandwiches, or poached eggs on toast?" her friend quipped.

"Be serious. This is lunch for a bishop, not a toddler, remember?"

And then, Jean Lund had an inspiration that completely solved the menu problem for Ellen. "You make the best chicken salad in town. Why not have that, hot rolls, iced tea, strawberries with powdered sugar, and brownies from the bakery for dessert?"

So, it was settled. The menu was, anyway. Finding an unstained tablecloth proved to be as much of a challenge as the menu selection had been. Eventually, the best of the lot became usable with the addition of doilies at each place.

But things began to happen. The Holts' refrigerator started making loud, grating noises. It seemed to gasp for the very breath of life, and finally expired. A new box was ordered promptly, arriving on Friday, before Tuesday's big event. On Saturday, the garbage disposal simply refused to dispose, and that too, required replacement. Surely, nothing else could go wrong.

And hardly anything else did. That is, if you could discount a flat tire on the way to the market on Monday morning, an ever-so-slight flooding of the Holts' basement after a hard rain that afternoon, and Ellen's chipping a front tooth, followed by a hasty trip to the dentist for temporary repair.

With the whole day taken up by a series of frustrating mishaps, Ellen was burning the midnight oil that night, cooking the breasts of chicken, chilling them so they could be finely diced early Tuesday morning.

Despite all the little inconveniences, Ellen Holt remained surprisingly calm. She awoke on Tuesday with a positive attitude, and in a short time, everything was ready for guests. The house was sparkling clean, the table had been set with polished silver, and the florist arrived with a centerpiece of fresh yellow and white daisies. The salad had been assembled, the strawberries were prepared for last minute placement in the best crystal bowl, butter rested in its silver dish, and iced tea had been made, all by 10:00 a.m.

Even after a leisurely bath and careful selection of a suitable dress for the occasion, Ellen was ready by 11:00. The Comptons were to arrive about noon. At 11:30, the telephone rang.

"Mrs. Holt?" a cultured voice spoke. "Cal Compton here. I'm sorry, but Susan and I will be just a bit later than we planned, more like 1:00 p.m. I imagine. I hope that won't inconvenience you too much."

"Not at all, Bishop Compton, we'll be happy to see you both when you get here," Ellen said, adding, "Drive carefully, and bring good appetites."

"You're very kind," the bishop said. "We'll be there as soon as possible."

Ellen made a couple of quick calls to the Stones and to her husband's office advising everyone of the time change.

Jim Holt and the Stones arrived together at 12:30. The Rev. Stone was especially interested in meeting Bishop Compton, an authority figure outside his own diocese, who might offer some helpful advice for a young Episcopal priest trying to decide whether or not to stay in his present parish.

It would be another hour though, before Bishop and Mrs. Compton arrived. It seems that they had taken a wrong turn somewhere.

By this time, everyone was very hungry. After exchanging a few pleasantries, the Comptons still had nothing but a vague recollection of ever having met the Holts. Ellen excused herself, left the guests to sipping sherry, and moved to the kitchen. There she put the finishing touches on what was destined to be a most remarkable luncheon.

Judging from the animated conversation and laughter from the living room, the Stones and the Comptons were hitting it off very well. Ellen poured the iced tea into chilled glasses, put the rolls in the oven to heat, and transferred whole strawberries to her great-grandmother's lovely crystal bowl. Then, she placed large lettuce leaves on each plate. She would summon her guests to the dining room for the blessing, and then return to the kitchen to place generous scoops of her famous chicken salad on the plates.

The bishop said the blessing, and Marcia Stone moved to the kitchen to help Ellen. But, as the first plate was being served, Susan Compton appeared. "Is there mayonnaise in the salad?" she asked in a soft voice. It should have sent up a red flag, but didn't.

"Yes," Ellen said, and then soon wished she were anywhere but where she was, after hearing the difference it made.

"The bishop can't tolerate mayonnaise," Mrs. Compton said.

"What can I fix for him?" Ellen asked, hoping her voice didn't betray her desperation.

"A peanut butter sandwich would be fine."

"What else?" Ellen asked, since she knew there was no peanut butter in the house.

"A poached egg on toast." Déjà vu. No. This couldn't have happened before. But, why did the conversation sound so familiar?

Ellen said a silent prayer. She hadn't bought eggs for several days, and had no idea if any were left. Opening the refrigerator ever so gingerly, she peered inside. "Thank you, thank you, thank you, God." For there, resting in the egg tray, was one solitary egg. Yes! One egg for the bishop's lunch.

She found the egg poacher, flipped a slice of bread into the toaster, and soon had the poached egg and lightly toasted bread placed on a plate in front of Bishop Compton.

The bishop couldn't eat the strawberries or brownies, but everyone else raved about them as well as the famous chicken salad with mayonnaise. Ellen shuddered to think what she would have done had there not been an egg in that tray. Imagine: one egg saved the day.

It remained a mystery why Susan Compton never mentioned her husband's dietary restrictions until the last minute.

Sometime later, after all the guests had gone, and Ellen was reviewing the day's events while loading the dishwasher, she suddenly burst into hysterical laughter.

Jim, fearing the worst, that Ellen had gone off the deep end following the stress of entertaining a prominent bishop, ran into the kitchen, prepared to dial 911, if necessary.

When she was finally able to stop laughing, Ellen explained what happened. "Peanut butter sandwiches or poached eggs on toast were two of the menus Jean Lund suggested the day we all got together. She was being silly, of course. But, look how it turned out! And, I'll bet Jean never thought of herself as a prophet."

Ellen could hardly wait to tell her friends what happened. As soon as the kitchen was cleaned up, she invited all of them to eat leftover chicken salad the next day. The big topic of conversation surely would be the bishop's light lunch.

CANDACE FACES LIFE

"**H**old onto your purse. Don't talk to strangers." Candace "Candy" Goldman's mother, Sadie, barked out orders as she hugged her daughter, who was about to board a Greyhound bus headed for a summer job in Vermont.

Bernie Goldman, Candy's father, simply pressed some crisp bills into her hand. "A little extra, just in case," he said.

Candy loved her parents—her mother, an 85 pound dynamo, who stood a couple of inches under five feet tall; and her father, a tall, quiet, dignified man, who was a chiropractor in the small town of Pittsford, New York.

Some people thought that Candy was unfortunate—having inherited her father's large-boned frame and wiry hair, and her mother's plain features. But as an only child in a financially comfortable family, she enjoyed many cultural advantages such as concerts, art classes, and memorable vacations.

Candy's character generally was beyond reproach, but she practiced one deception, and it concerned her religion. Every

Saturday, from the time she was 12 until she was 15, her parents had sent her to Hebrew School at the B'Nai Brith Temple in Rochester. She never attended. As soon as the bus reached the city depot, Candy headed for the movie theaters, using the lunch money her parents had given her to indulge her cravings for the fruits of the silver screen.

She memorized dialogue, especially between her favorite actors, Katharine Hepburn and Spencer Tracy. Back home in her bedroom, she replayed romantic scenes in front of the mirror, imagining with half-closed eyes that she resembled Miss Hepburn.

This dramatic flair found expression in conversations with friends. A vacation in Philadelphia, highlighted by a ride in her cousin's new convertible, was translated: "We went for a spin in his roadster." Following a family trip to New York City for a chiropractic convention, Candy announced, "We took tea at the Algonquin." And of course, the Goldmans "dined al fresco at Cape Cod."

Now, Candy was going to Brattleboro, Vermont to work as a waitress at the Mountain View Inn until mid-August, before entering the University of Chicago.

The bus driver was taking tickets and helping passengers up the steps. Candy found a window seat and settled down comfortably. Soon, the door closed, and the driver slowly backed the bus out of its parking space. Candy rubbed the window pane with a tissue to get a clearer view of her parents standing close together, waving and looking a little sad.

A thin young woman with stringy, long blonde hair suddenly appeared. "Okay if I sit here?" she asked.

"Oh sure," Candy said. "How far are you going?"

"Syracuse. I'm gonna live with my sister and get a job in the city."

Candy noticed that the girl, who wore a faded print skirt and a shabby peasant blouse, was young, maybe 15. "Where's your home?" she asked.

"Buffalo. Mom's remarried. Her new husband's a dumb jerk. I've been visiting my cousin in Rochester."

"You'll go to school in Syracuse?" Candy asked.

"Are you kidding? I quit. I wanna get married and have kids. I'm gonna work at Grant's."

Candy closed her eyes. Conversation with the high school dropout was becoming boring. The steady drone of the motor as the bus sped through the dark night, lulled her to sleep.

It seemed that only a few minutes had passed before the driver announced, "Syracuse. There'll be a thirty-five minute stop for passengers continuing to Albany. Restrooms and lunch counter are in the terminal. This is bus number 7, gate 10. Take all personal items with you. Be back on time, please."

The young woman who had been sitting next to Candy now stood by the door, ready to be among the first off the bus.

At the lunch counter, Candy ordered a chocolate soda, but when she opened her purse to pay, she realized that her wallet was missing. "That girl must have taken it while I slept," she thought.

Candy found enough coins in a change purse to cover the soda, then asked directions to the nearest policeman.

She raced up the stairs, bursting into an office marked "Security," where a portly, balding, middle-aged man sat smoking a cigar and reading a magazine. A half-full cup of coffee, a tin can serving as an ashtray, and a telephone were the only items on the desk, in addition to the man's feet.

"Somebody took your purse?" the man asked.

"No, my wallet, on the bus from Rochester, while I was asleep. She was a thin, stringy-haired blonde, about 15, wearing a printed skirt and a white peasant blouse. She said she was going to live with her sister in Syracuse and work at Grant's. I'm on my way to Brattleboro, and have to catch a bus in fifteen minutes. Please, find her! I'm practically broke." Candy suddenly remembered the money her father had given her before she left, and which she now felt in the pocket of her jacket.

"Probably long gone by now," the detective said. "Name?"

"Candy. Candace Goldman, from Pittsford."

"Name of alleged thief?"

"Alleged? She took it all right, but I don't know her name."

"Fill out this form," the detective said, handing it over without lifting his eyes from the magazine.

"Aren't you going to look for the girl now?"

"Wouldn't do any good. Put down your telephone number. We'll be in touch," the man promised.

Candy completed the form. She raced down the steps to gate 10, and boarded just as the bus was about to leave. She found an empty seat in the back, and then counted the money in her pocket. Five ones and a five. *That'll go a long way*, she thought.

In Albany, Candy changed buses, and a few hours later, arrived in Brattleboro, where she awaited the Mountain View Inn's station wagon.

Soon, a bus arrived from New York, and a tall, well-tanned man got off. He wore sun glasses and carried a camera bag. The sleeves of his open-necked blue oxford shirt were rolled up just below the elbow, revealing muscular, hairy arms. A khaki vest covered with pockets, light-colored trousers, and hiking boots completed his outfit.

A hunk, maybe a journalist, Candy imagined. Brushing straight black hair from his forehead, he looked around, and then headed for the bench where Candy sat.

"Pardon me, miss, do you know if the Mountain View Inn taxi has been here?" he asked.

In a squeaky voice, Candy answered, "Not yet. I'm waiting for it, though."

The young man stuck out his hand. "Alec LeBeau. Glad to meet you. I'm staying at the inn for a night before heading north."

Later, Candy would wonder why she invented the outlandish story she told him, but the words came out so easily.

"Candace Goldman. I'm vacationing at Mountain View for the

summer and working on my doctoral thesis in theater arts history at the Sorbonne."

For a few uncomfortable moments, the young man didn't speak. He stared. He stood up, removed his sunglasses, stuck them in one of the vest pockets, and squinted. Then, he said, "You, my dear, are wasting your time studying history. Put it aside. Go to Hollywood for a screen test. You are blessed with a perfect face, the perfect type in fact, for a movie a friend and I are making for MGM. I can't believe it. My first week talent scouting, and I've found the ONE!"

"But, I'm not an actress," Candy protested.

"Don't worry, we can teach you whatever you need to know," Alec assured her.

"What do you suggest?" Candy wanted to know.

"As soon as you get to the inn, call the number on my business card. Tell the secretary that Alec LeBeau wants you to take a screen test as soon as possible. Right now, I'd like some stills of you for publicity purposes."

Candy posed, and Alec clicked away until the wagon arrived from the inn. En route, he outlined the screen play. It was about a college student who falls in love with a professional golfer, leaves school to follow his tour, and discovers that the golfer is married and that his wife is a paraplegic, the result of an accident caused by his drunken driving.

Candy would portray the student. By the time they arrived at the inn, she was sold on a movie career. The two agreed to meet at breakfast the next morning to make arrangements for the California trip.

From her room, Candy dialed the number on Alec's card. A voice answered, "Metro Screen, Elaine Jenkins speaking."

"This is Candace Goldman. Alec LeBeau asked me to make an appointment for a screen test. He wants me to try out for the part of Joyce Elliot in 'Sand Trap.'"

"Did he tell you that you're perfect for the new film?"

"Yes!"

"Oh, oh. Alec's up to his old tricks, playing the movie mogul. I'm sorry. Alec is the son of Metro's owner. We custom make window and door screens, screening for porches, that type of thing. Alec thinks it's amusing to pose as a talent scout and recruit actors for screen tests."

Candy's chin dropped. Her eyes filled with tears. *I never doubted him*, she thought. *How could I have been so gullible?*

Exhausted, she lay down on the bed and fell asleep, awakening when the telephone rang. It was the detective from Syracuse. "We found your wallet, miss. We'll send it special delivery."

"Did you arrest the girl?" Candy asked.

"No. We tracked her down, but she didn't take it. The wallet was discovered on the floor of the bus at Albany by the driver."

RECIPE FOR SLANDER

The postman's arrival, signaled by two toots on the horn of a well-worn Jeep, once brought Ann Hoffman eagerly to the mailbox at the end of her driveway. But, for the past two weeks, the sound had assumed an annoying, even ominous character. Mixed in with bills, advertisements, invitations to weddings, and an appointment reminder from her dentist, there were the poison pen letters.

Written in green ink, the cryptic messages each began the same way: "My dear, what I have to tell you is something I regret doing, but someone must—it's for your own good."

The subject was Ann's husband, Tom, suggesting that he and a recent divorcee, his secretary in the law practice, were having a torrid love affair. According to the anonymous writer, everyone in the small town of Clear Springs, New York, knew about it. Everyone, of course, but Ann.

The Hoffmans had been married for fifteen wonderful years, or so Ann believed that they were. They had met in college, and married the summer Tom graduated from law school. Ann had worked as his secretary in a practice he then shared with his father. When their first child, Jeanmarie, was born the following year, Ann stayed home to be a full-time mother. Two years later, the twins, Mark and Alan, were born, and since then, Ann had given up any thoughts of working outside her home.

Ann's days were filled with caring for children and home, gardening, volunteering at the local hospital one day a week, and doing church work. The petite redhead with the infectious laugh and easy manner was a popular figure in the community.

Tom's practice had grown with the town's population, and since the death of his father last year, he was handling all the cases himself. There were some late evenings spent at the office in recent months, but until the arrival of that first letter, Ann had not been suspicious. Now, she found herself questioning her husband's every move, examining his shirts and handkerchiefs for possible lipstick stains, and stopping by his office more frequently.

At first, Tom seemed pleased to see her when she dropped in unannounced. "Nothing's better than a visit from my favorite redhead," he'd insisted when she asked if he minded the impromptu visits. A couple of times he had taken her to lunch. But, the last time, she had sensed his impatience. Perhaps it was only her imagination.

Why don't I show him the letters, ask him about the affair? Ann questioned herself. But something was holding her back. Maybe the accusation was true; maybe she feared knowing the truth.

Ann could take the letters to the police, but what could they do— follow everyone who mailed a letter? If they asked for a list of enemies, it wouldn't contain a single name. Ann considered all the townspeople as friends. Even Tom's secretary, the alleged scarlet woman, seemed an unlikely prospect for an affair with her boss. The model of a conservative office employee, Lauren Baxter was plain-faced and matronly, devoted to her only child, a teen-aged girl, Kim, who was grateful when her mother divorced her abusive, alcoholic father.

The letters kept coming, and now, after number five, Ann decided that she, and she alone, would have to solve the mystery of the anonymous writer and the allegation of her husband's unfaithfulness.

Ann began by assembling all the letters and taking a closer look at the writing rather than the content, to see if there was a recognizable pattern, a clue, anything that might be helpful.

At first, there was nothing, except that her eyes became tired, focusing on that awful green ink. Her head ached. But finally, Ann noticed that the writer had an odd way of using an apostrophe, giving it a backwards slant in words like can't and won't.

Systematically, Ann began going over the names of people she knew, separating them first into lists under categories such as church, PTA, hospital volunteers, garden club members, and so forth. She could eliminate several names from each group whose handwriting she never had seen.

But there was one name that kept popping up—Margie Burns— former president of the gourmet cooking group Ann belonged to. Ann recalled that there was something unusual about her writing. Frantically, she began checking her recipe file, but she found nothing handwritten by Mrs. Burns, although several of her typed recipes were there.

Ann was unsure how to proceed, until the twins accidentally provided a perfect way. The boys were busy after school that day, doing their homework for the first-aid class they were taking to earn badges in Boy Scouts. Mark was using Alan as his victim, practicing tying a sling for a sprained arm.

Observing this activity, Ann thought of having one of the children visit Mrs. Burns and having her write out a recipe.

Ann decided to confide in daughter, Jeanmarie, whose talent for acting, (leads in all the school plays), would now have a practical application. Jeanmarie's reaction was typical. She bubbled with enthusiasm. "Gee Mom, this is so cool. You get to play Jessica Fletcher, and I'm your assistant. Let's do it!"

Mark got more practice applying a sling to Jeanmarie's writing arm, and she was soon off to the Burns's house armed with a recipe card and a sad story about having sprained her arm in gym class.

Getting Mrs. Burns to write out her famous state fair prize-winning recipe for Triple Jeopardy Chocolate Fudge Brownies was a snap.

Back home, comparing the handwriting, even for amateurs, presented no challenge. It was exactly the same as the poison pen letters, including the backward slanted apostrophes. The biggest question was, "Why would Margie Burns write those letters?" Perhaps the woman still carried a grudge about a civil suit she once lost to a neighbor Tom had represented. Ann turned over all the evidence to Tom. After all, this was a case for her favorite attorney.

ABOUT THE AUTHOR

Photo by Kathryn Lauer.

Nancy Wiedman grew up in Western New York State.

She is a graduate of Goddard College, Plainfield, Vermont.

Her career experience includes time spent as an executive secretary, teaching high school English, and finally, working as a columnist, staff reporter/photographer for a weekly newspaper. She has won press awards for column and feature writing in Kentucky, and a Metro Louisville Award as part of a team in 1990.

Nancy lives in Tucson, Arizona.

www.ingramcontent.com/pod-product-compliance
Lightning Source LLC
Chambersburg PA
CBHW022052170626
46808CB00003B/1448